Timeless Fairy Tales

Goldilocks and the Three Bears

AWARD PUBLICATIONS LIMITED

There was once a little girl called Goldilocks. She loved to go exploring in the woods near her home, and one morning as she walked a delicious smell wafted her way.

"Mmm," said Goldilocks. "Someone is cooking porridge!" Goldilocks loved porridge.

Now, three bears lived in the wood: a great big Father Bear, a middle-sized Mother Bear and a tiny little Baby Bear. It was their porridge Goldilocks could smell.

It was much too hot so Father Bear said, "Let's go for a nice walk. When we get back the porridge will be ready to eat."

So off they went.

A few moments later, Goldilocks arrived at the hollow tree where the bears lived.

Goldilocks had never seen a front door in a tree before. She was so curious, that she opened the door and stepped inside…

…into in a cosy
little kitchen, where
three bowls of porridge
were set on the table.
A great big bowl.
A middle-sized bowl.
And a tiny little bowl.

The steaming bowls of porridge made Goldilocks feel very hungry. So hungry, that she tried a spoonful of the porridge from the great big bowl. Ouch! It was much too hot!

Next, she tried the middle-sized bowl. But this porridge was too cold.

Last of all, Goldilocks tried the porridge in the tiny little bowl.

It was just right. In fact, Goldilocks liked it so much that she ate it all up!

Eating all that porridge made Goldilocks very sleepy.

She wandered into the next room and saw a great big chair.

"I'm so tired," sighed Goldilocks. "I think I'll sit down for a while." But the big chair was Father Bear's chair. It was far too big, and not at all comfy.

"This chair's much too soft!" said Goldilocks.

Goldilocks tried the middle-sized chair next. It was Mother Bear's chair. It was close to a window with a lovely view of the woods.

"I'd like to sit here," said Goldilocks. "I can look out of the window." But when she sat on the middle-sized chair, she found that it wasn't at all comfy.

"Oh dear!" said Goldilocks. "This chair's much too hard."

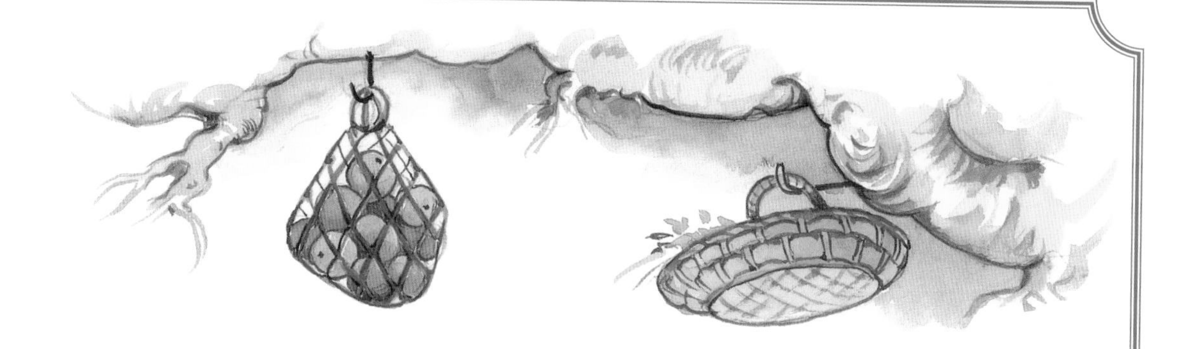

Then Goldilocks spotted a tiny little green chair, with a pretty checked cushion. This chair was just right.

But Goldilocks was too heavy for the little chair…

…and one of its legs snapped off, tipping her onto the floor!

Goldilocks picked herself up and decided to explore upstairs. “Maybe I can find somewhere to rest up here,” she thought.

At the top of the stairs, Goldilocks came to a green door. By now she was feeling very sleepy indeed. All she wanted to do was lie down and rest.

Cautiously, Goldilocks opened the door. Inside the room were three lovely, wooden beds: a great big bed, a middle-sized bed and a tiny little bed. They all looked so very comfortable.

Each was covered in a beautiful quilt, and they were neatly made up, just ready for a tired little girl to jump into.

Goldilocks tried the great big bed first, but it was much too soft.

Then she tried the middle-sized bed. But it was too hard.

Finally, Goldilocks lay down on the tiny little bed. It was just right! As soon as her head touched the pillow, Goldilocks fell into a deep sleep.

By now, the three bears were on their way home. They were all looking forward to their breakfast.

But when they stepped inside the door, they had a surprise.

"Someone's been eating my porridge!" exclaimed great big Father Bear.

"And someone's been eating *my* porridge!" said middle-sized Mother Bear.

"And someone's been eating *my* porridge," squeaked tiny little Baby Bear, "and they've eaten it all up!"

The three bears went into the next room.

"Someone has been sitting in my chair!" growled great big Father Bear.

"And someone's been sitting in *my* chair, too," said middle-sized Mother Bear.

"Oh!" cried tiny little Baby Bear. "Someone has been sitting in *my* chair. And they've broken it!"

The three bears were gathered round Baby Bear's broken chair when, suddenly, Father Bear heard a noise upstairs.

"Maybe whoever it is has not left yet!" growled Father Bear as he noticed the open door at the top of the stairs.

The three bears quietly climbed the stairs, wondering what they might find.

"Someone's been sleeping in my bed," said great big Father Bear, crossly.

"And someone's been sleeping in *my* bed!" complained middle-sized Mother Bear.

"And someone's been sleeping in *my* bed," squeaked tiny little Baby Bear, "AND SHE'S STILL HERE!"

Goldilocks woke with a start. She took one look at the bears and screamed in fright.

Then she leapt out of the bed, fled past the astonished bears and ran down the stairs.

The three bears tumbled after her.

But Goldilocks ran, and ran, and ran, as fast as her legs could carry her.

She didn't stop running until she was nearly home.

As for the three bears, well, they never saw Goldilocks ever again.

THE END

Timeless Fairy Tales

Classic stories are brought magically to life in this beautifully illustrated collectable library of easy-to-read traditional fairy tales.

Titles in the series:

Cinderella
Puss in Boots
The Ugly Duckling
The Little Tin Soldier
Little Red Riding Hood
Goldilocks and the Three Bears
The Adventures of Tom Thumb
Snow White and the Seven Dwarfs
Aladdin and His Magical Lamp
Jack and the Beanstalk
The Three Little Pigs
Pinocchio

ISBN 978-1-84135-536-8

First published 2008

Published by Award Publications Limited,
The Old Riding School, The Welbeck Estate,
Worksop, Nottinghamshire, S80 3LR

11 3

Printed in China

ap
award publications limited